# ABOUT THE

David Mason, born 196 Manchester University before sales training with a large pharmaceutical company. From 1992 to 2000 he ran his own restaurant - Alfresco Eating House whilst working at schools and giving live poetry performances.

He is now a full-time writer and visits many schools to run Creative Writing and Poetry Workshops. Please contact him at the address overleaf if you would like him to appear at a school or venue near you.

## ABOUT THE ILLUSTRATOR

Nick Walmsley, also born 1960, divides his time between art, illustration and music (as an organist): he also writes and lectures on airship history. He is Visiting Artist to various aviation bodies, edits the international journal "Dirigible" for the Airship Heritage Trust, and his book "R101 - a Pictorial History" was published in October 2000.

Other interests include life and culture in the Mediterranean and the Balkans. An interest in vintage cars means that he can generally be found relaxing with his 1931 Austin 7!

"The Elf who sang the King to sleep" © David J. Mason 2002
Publishing address: North Street Publishing, 1 North Street, North Walsham Norfolk
NR28 9DH
Telephone 01692 406877 DavidMasonPoet@AOL.com

Illustrations © Nick Walmsley 2002
Contact address: Tryddyn, Horning Road West, Hoveton, Norfolk NR12 8QJ
Telephone 01603 782758

British Library Cataloguing-in-Publication Data
A Catalogue record for this book is available from the British Library
David J. Mason
ISBN 09521326 9 9

**By the same author:**

| | |
|---|---|
| "Inside Out" | Poetry by David J. Mason published 1996 |
| "Speaking Out" | Audio collection of selected work from "Inside Out"and "Get a Life" |
| "Get a Life" | Poetry collection published in 1997; illustrated by Nick Walmsley |
| "Seven Summers" | Poetry collection published in 1998 |
| "Leo's Magic Shoes" | Children's novel published in 1999; illustrated by Kirsty Munro. *Reprinted as* "Pedro's Magic Shoes" in 2000 with illustrations by Nick Walmsley |
| "The Great Sweetshop Robbery and Other Poems" | Children's Poetry Collection published 2001 |
| "Handy Andy has the candy" | Children's Poetry Collection published 2001 |
| "Go Teddy go" | Children's CD poetry-song collection released 2002 |

*Produced by* Skippers Print & Design
53a The Green, Martham, Great Yarmouth, Norfolk NR29 4PF
Telephone: 01493 740998

This book is dedicated to all my family as together
we now make seven:
Helen, Abbey, Leo, Rosa, Rory and Lily.


Once again, thanks to Nick: our illustrator,
proof-reader and creative counsellor!

# CONTENTS

# THE ELF WHO SANG THE KING TO SLEEP

## NEW FABLES AND FAIRY TALES

By David J. Mason

Illustrated by Nick Walmsley

# THE ELF WHO SANG THE KING TO SLEEP

## I

A long time ago, there lived an elf who possessed the most wonderful singing voice in the whole of Elfdom. How he came to have it was a mystery to the rest of the elves. Some said that he was really an elf bird. Others, who were jealous, claimed that he had stolen the songs from the gods and that his voice was not his own.

His mother, of course, knew why he sang so. It was because she had sung to him when he was a young elf. Her lullabies and traditional elf-tales had found their way through his ears and into his head. Sometime later they were released through his mouth, matured like a fine wine, improved with the years.

Whatever the reason for his voice, the elf loved to sing, new songs and old. He also loved to entertain - not because he was a boastful, conceited little elf - but because he loved to bring pleasure to his listeners. Indeed, he was more than a little embarrassed if complimented on his art. He would shrug his shoulders and say that every elf was good at something: he just happened to have a good voice. Then he would give the glory to his mother and her friends who were the *real* singers and who had taught him everything he knew.

The elf, whose name was Fynn, held no greater ambition than to perform his songs for as wide an audience as possible. He had no other interest in life. He did not care for riches or status. He simply wanted to sing to the world. So one day he determined to visit the King of the Elves to see what he should do to realise his dream.

When Fynn arrived for his audience with the King of the Elves, he was surprised to learn that the King had heard of his singing: his reputation had clearly preceded him.

"You may, of course, sing throughout the whole of Elfdom, should you so desire," said the King. "But let me warn you there will be those jealous of your talent who will not appreciate you. They will say, behind your back (and sometimes to your face) that you are a very ordinary elf, and that nothing of extraordinary value could possibly come from a brother elf."

The King of the Elves continued, "You have, as I see it, but one choice if you sincerely wish to entertain a truly appreciative audience."

"What is that?" asked Fynn, quietly.

"You must travel: one is not always appreciated in his own land. You must travel to another Kingdom, a Kingdom of people. There, I think, you will find true lovers of your song."

"Then, though I am deeply afraid of leaving my home and all I know, I must travel," said Fynn.

So it was that Fynn left that very same night on his long journey across Elfdom to reach the next Kingdom. He left with tears in his eyes, a lump in his throat and a frightening question at the back of his mind: would he ever return to his homeland?

## II

Fynn had been travelling a long time; he had lost count of the days and weeks but once on his way, with his mind made up, he really rather enjoyed his journeying. The walking gave a rhythm to his mind and made for good singing. He sang of everything he saw, and of all the thoughts that came into his mind. His songs were joyful and loud, soft and reflective. They were old and yet they were new.

The landscape about him changed very little, and it was only when he remembered that he had not seen another elf for quite some days that he realised he must have crossed over into some other Kingdom.

How far would he have to travel before he met human beings? He had no idea.

At length, he came upon one of a series of streams flowing through the most beautiful meadows imaginable. All about him stood long grasses and woven between the tussocks, lay patches of strikingly rich-coloured wild flowers of red, white and yellow.

"What a heavenly place this is!" whispered Fynn to himself, so as not to disturb the calm all about him.

Suddenly, Fynn heard the sound of footsteps approaching and quickly hid behind a huge bush, a mass of red bell-shaped flowers. He peeped between the branches and caught sight of a human being, a young maiden, humming gently to herself and smiling. She was picking posies of flowers and carefully placing them in a wicker basket.

"Excuse me," said Fynn, "I don't want to frighten you, but I'm so glad to have met someone at long last."

The girl, after recovering from the initial shock of meeting Fynn the elf, listened intently to what he had to say.

Fynn told her of his dream and his journey, and asked

if he might sing to her. She agreed without hesitation, delighted that she should be the first human being to hear Fynn's song.

So he sang to her and immediately she was transfixed by the beauty of the sound. When he had finished, she sat entranced and after some time, asked if he would sing again. Thus Fynn had made a friend of the girl, who was so impressed by his singing that she exclaimed, "Come with me, let us not waste a minute. Come with me to see our King. There you will have the biggest and most kindly audience you can imagine. I'm sure he and the people will love you. Do come, please!"

Fynn nodded. He was delighted with this sudden invitation.

"How far must we journey?" he asked.

"It is a long walk from here. I come this way only once in a while to pick the summer flowers. Fynn noticed she was fidgeting, eager to be on her way.

"It will be dark soon; we should rest until daylight," Fynn reasoned.

The girl giggled and tugged at Fynn's arm.

"Quick come," she said, "there is no darkness in this Kingdom; you must be thinking of another. Here there is no night at all."

Fynn thought hard. He remembered not resting for a long time, nor seeing darkness. He must have crossed over into a new Kingdom, this strange Kingdom, without knowing it.

Fynn was being pulled along. It seemed the girl had no more time for questions, walking, almost running, towards her people. The pace was exhausting. Never before had Fynn been so glad to reach a destination.

"Come straight away. I shall introduce you to my family and friends to begin with and you shall sing to them. Soon afterwards, you shall see the King. Hurry, I am so excited!"

The girl led the way through the city gates, moving as swiftly as ever. There were crowds of people rushing up and down the street, some with parcels but most empty-handed, all scurrying and weaving this way and that way.

Fynn found all this movement rather alarming. He had to dodge the oncoming people to avoid being squashed several times. There was noise too, ceaseless noise: clatter, shouts, people pointing and waving. Fynn noticed that hardly anyone stood still. The girl Lily, as she was called, suddenly stopped dead in front of him and banged on a colourful yellow door that opened out on to this pedestrian highway. She shifted from one foot to the other, waiting for an answer, which was not long in coming. There was an embrace, an introduction to Fynn, a nod, some smiles, the tapping of feet and, within seconds, Fynn found himself singing.

All at once, Lily and her family fell under the spell of Fynn's voice. They seemed to fall into a dream, their eyes glazing over, their jerky bodies still, their twitching muscles relaxed, their worried frowns gone and replaced with satisfied smiles. Fynn continued and, as long as he sang, so his audience continued to dream.

When he finished, they would sit up with a start but then melt back into dreamland when he began again. However, Fynn could not continue for long as he was drained of energy after the journey. He must stop for a rest: a sleep was what he really wanted.

Fynn noticed that Lily was bursting with life. She and her family, just like all the others in the street, could simply not sit still. They were overloaded with nervous energy. Fynn decided he must ask a few questions of Lily to try and understand the nature of this strange people. They were friendly enough; there was no question of their good intentions, but their nervousness was more than Fynn could stand. He himself was beginning to feel unbearably edgy in their company.

On hearing his questions, Lily decided she must take him aside to another room where she could explain all. It was simple, she told him. Without darkness, in a kingdom such as theirs, people would sleep very little: one hour in every twenty-four, perhaps less. The daylight gave energy - so much that the people were constantly full of it and needing to rid themselves of it. That was why, she told Fynn, that everyone was used to the behaviour. It seemed normal to be nervous.

"You are not nervous when I sing," suggested Fynn.

"No, your singing gives us rest and it is good for us to rest for a few more minutes. See how wonderful your songs are that they can soothe even ourselves!"

"Don't you want darkness? That would bring you proper rest. You would never again have to rush around like you do, wasting all this hard work and achieving nothing."

Lily looked sad at his words.

"It is not our doing. It is the King's. We should all like to move from here to another Kingdom where we can sleep but the King has forbidden it."

"Why? Why will he not let you sleep? Everyone has to sleep!" protested Fynn.

"We must not sleep… for sleep is dangerous."

"Dangerous?" Fynn could not believe what he was hearing.

"Yes, dangerous! Let me tell you. Our ancestors once lived in the next Kingdom to here. There, things were different: there was darkness, there was sleep and rest, there was art and music, singing, dancing and thinking. There was time for all of this. People did not rush; people worked only when necessary.

"Then, one terrible night, when the people were sleeping soundly, there came invaders: an angry tribe of conquerors. They drove the people from the city out into the wilderness and took all the houses and belongings, leaving our ancestors with nothing. Because of our nature, our ancestors did not fight. They

13

were a peaceful, thoughtful people who had no time for arguing with others.

"So they spent many months wandering and during that time their leader died and a new King was needed. He was a very young King, inexperienced in the ways of ruling and he blamed his people for the shame they had brought upon themselves. He did not understand the true beauty of their nature. He swore that they would never be caught napping again.

"The King of whom I speak is the very same King who rules now. He is much older of course, but still as determined as ever. Imagine his delight when he came upon the Kingdom in which we now live. While others yearn for the darkness of old, the young King was delighted to have found a place where he could rule safe in the knowledge that daylight would always be, and his people could never again be attacked in the dark. Even now, he still demands vigilance at every hour and his continued warnings make our nervous condition even worse.

"Our King is happy here. Even though he cannot rest, he knows we are safe from attack. He would never consider moving to another kingdom where darkness might fall and danger arise."

Fynn understood everything. Lily and her people were trapped.

"Please Fynn, do not leave us. More than anyone else, we need the few moments of rest you bring with your songs. You have found your dream audience, and we have found our little dreams."

"Tomorrow then I will take you to see the King. You will be able to give him the rest he needs. He has slept so few hours in these many years that he is very irritable. Only you can calm him.

"As for now, you must rest; sleep, if you need to. However, you will find, as we did, that the longer you stay here the less you will sleep."

Fynn, left alone in the room, pondered on her words. He knew he could not stay as she had pleaded. If he could not rest then he would not be able to sing or make tunes and his voice would shrivel. He would become restless and waste his time busying himself like Lily and her people. Yes, he was sad for them, but he would return to Elfdom and rest. First though, he must answer some of Lily's pleas and sing for the King. It would bring great pleasure to himself and his audience. This was why he had made the journey after all, was it not? Besides, there could be no danger in such an exercise... could there?

## III

Fynn found sleeping very difficult. The little room, bare except for the bed with its soft feather mattress, was very dark; but Fynn knew that outside the house it was light. Hadn't he slept the day before? Why, he had snoozed by the side of rivers and pools, laid his head down under huge friendly trees, sheltered and dozed under massive fortress rocks. If he was able to sleep during the day then, why not now? He was so tired, he reasoned, that perhaps he was *too* tired. No, he considered it must be this place, this Kingdom where everyone and everything was so busy. Fynn was sure that if the noise, the hustle and bustle outside suddenly stopped, then he would be able to sleep. This, of course, was never going to happen.

Fynn tossed and turned, lay on his back, on his front, on his side, then on his back again. He sighed and pretended to snore to send his body to sleep. Still his mind would not rest. At long last he was able to fall into a fitful dreamland by imagining he was back in Elfdom, sleeping out in the dark amongst the fragrant bushes, alongside the dripping waterfalls and deep, clear pools. It was a balmy summer's night; the stars winked and the moon yawned. The peaceful earth swallowed the little elf as he nestled against it. He sank into soft slumber.

He was awoken by a firm knocking on the door. Before he had time to answer, Lily strode into the room. Without waiting, she began, "I hope you are rested. I have been to see the King's personal adviser. He is extremely interested. He thinks the King will be very pleased to hear your song. You must come to see the King now."

Fynn sat up, rubbing his eyes, trying to listen and make sense of all that Lily was telling him.

"One question if you please, Lily," he said, "How long have I been asleep? I feel as if I have hardly slept."

"I cannot be sure how long you have slept," answered Lily, in a matter-of-fact way.

"How many hours, roughly speaking?" asked Fynn again.

"Hours? I do not know how many hours," Lily chuckled. "We have given up telling time here. There are no timepieces to mark the passing of time."

"Why?" asked Fynn. "Does nobody care?"

"Here, there is no darkness and the sun does not move in the sky – it is always in the middle, neither too high nor too low, neither too hot nor too cold. If the sun does not move, then there is not need for us to check the movement of time. We only know of time passing because we grow older; some die and some are born. All our mornings, lunchtimes, afternoons, teatimes, evenings and nighttimes merge into one continuous day during which we are continuously active, apart from a few minutes here and there."

"I see," said Fynn, trying to imagine a life with no beginning, middle and end except the one day on which you were born and the one day on which you would die. Between those two extremes lay a busy workload and, without rest, all to no purpose, it seemed. As he listed to Lily's explanation, his greatest desire was to return immediately to Elfdom. However, he could not disappoint Lily now. She seemed so absolutely sure that he must go with her and sing to the King.

"Now, please, I have answered enough questions

17

and the King is expecting you. We must not keep him waiting under any circumstances."

Lily pulled hard at Fynn's hand, tugging him through the door and out into the street. Nothing had changed from the moment Fynn had entered the city. There was still the same hustle and bustle, almost chaos, Fynn thought. He looked to the sun. It was as Lily had described: neither too high nor too low. It was the sun, Fynn thought, which gave the energy to these people, the very energy that made them frantic and denied them sleep.

The pair made their way to the palace. They dodged through the crowds who, it seemed to Fynn, were constantly running in circles. They passed the fidgety palace guards and found themselves outside the main throne room. Lily knocked hard and long. There was a hurried answer from within; it was, Lily said, the King's voice.

"Yes, yes I'm coming, I'm coming! Who is it, who is it? Won't be a second, won't be a second! Nearly there, nearly ... here we are!"

The King opened the door, invited the elf inside, and shut Lily out.

"Can't stand too many people about," he said grumpily.

The King would not, could not, sit down. His throne, situated in the middle of the room, looked as if it had never been sat upon. Instead, the King paced in circles around it, sometimes a little slower, sometimes a little faster.

After two complete circuits of the room, the King finally appeared to notice the presence of his guest. It was at that moment he finally stopped pacing. However, he could not remain still and, while he spoke or listened, would go through a varied routine of nervous trickery: Folding and unfolding of the arms, the hands in front or moved behind the back; the spreading and recoiling of fingers. At intervals, the King would bring himself up to his full height on tiptoe and then relax again with his feet firmly flat on the floor. Fynn noticed he would bang his ankles together, pull his shoulders back, lift his rib cage and tilt his head first to one side then to the other. If he did manage to look at Fynn, he would do so whilst raising alternate eyebrows, flexing each nostril in turn, pursing his lips, and then producing a madman's grin that occupied nearly half of his face.

Then there was the constant blinking that made Fynn feel very uncomfortable, so that in the end Fynn thought he had something stuck in his own eye and would rub it in response to the King's habit. Last of all, Fynn noticed the King's head which, when it wasn't leaning in one direction or the other, was always moving with a slight tremble as though he were suffering some nervous disease that made the head nod constantly.

Fynn tried not to stare lest he offend the King. However, it was very difficult not to, such behaviour being the strangest he had ever encountered.

After his pacing and during his twitching, the King spoke in abrupt tones.

"You are the elf, I see. You have a most wonderful voice. Your gift will soothe me, I am told. I need a little rest. I am old now. Sing then, I can't be hanging around waiting."

"Will you sit upon your throne, your Majesty, to listen?" enquired Fynn.

"Sit? No! Whatever is to be done is done standing! Now hurry!"

At once, Fynn began his song: an old elfin song of green trees, bushes and meadows of restful green. It told of how the Creator chose green as the colour of the country where all his creatures could roam and find peace in their surroundings. Fynn had sung that piece more times than he cared to remember, but each time it was as fresh as the first. The song brought back a feeling of solemn joy to his heart; a feeling that made its way to his voice and gave it a wondrous, happy, soothing tone. The words drifted from him as clouds moving lazily across a blue sky, like smoke from a warm friendly chimney on a cold frosty day.

The King fell under the spell of the music and the words. All parts of his body ceased their movement. His face relaxed and the twitching of the mouth, nose and eyes stopped. It was as if a new King stood before Fynn, younger in appearance, all anxiety drained away.

As the song continued, the King moved slowly, very slowly indeed, taking tiny, gentle steps in rhythm to the song. He was making his way towards the throne, the momentum of the song carrying him each step along the way. Like one who is sleepwalking, he glided on, his eyes wide open and unblinking. The King lowered himself on to his throne and nestled himself into its soft velvet cloth. As he snuggled down, his eyes closed tight shut and he slept as a baby might sleep. At long last he had found a resting place.

Fynn observed every detail of the King's behaviour. It was sometimes difficult to concentrate on his song at the same time but he did not want to miss a second of the sequence unfolding before him. This, Fynn considered, was his own dream come true – to be able to transform the appearance and behaviour of many, let alone a King, through the gift of his song. This one moment made all the endless hours, days, weeks and years of practice worthwhile. The song had shown itself to have power. Fynn was merely a vessel through which the power of the song might flow – he would never claim the power for himself. Yet, to think that he, an ordinary elf, had been chosen to bring this gift. A gift that was now so very much appreciated! Yes, he had seen the proof! Now Fynn was not so sure about wanting to return to Elfdom. After all, his was a gift that needed exercising again and again and again.

Fynn finished his song, but before he could move on to another, the King awoke. Startled to find himself sitting, he rose from his throne and began his pacing as if the few minutes sleep had given him even more energy.

"Thank you, thank you. Marvellous, wonderful! Wonderful, marvellous! The best, the greatest! The greatest the best! A gift from the gods! God's gift!" the King exclaimed.

Fynn bowed. He would have liked to have stayed and asked questions of the King, and perhaps have lingered a little longer and sung a little more. However, the King was in no mood for such things.

"You will come here again – soon!" the King commanded.

"When shall I come?" Fynn asked.

The King looked at the elf, perplexed.

"Soon, I have said, soon!" He spoke as though the elf lacked intelligence.

It was then that Fynn remembered there was no time in this Kingdom. To ask for a specific hours or day was, frankly, a waste of time. He could see that the King was becoming very impatient and wished to be rid of him and his silly questions.

"Goodbye," said the elf softly to the King. The King did not seem to notice Fynn's departure; he was once again pacing round and round his throne.

## IV

Fynn found that he began to develop a certain sense of the passing of time, so that he was able to estimate the time that the King had called 'soon'. This, according to Fynn, meant that 'soon' was 'daily'.

Fynn was given a room in Lily's family home and it was made quite clear from his conversation with the family that the elf was expected to stay. Although they had not said so directly, it was obvious that they did not expect Fynn to return to Elfdom.

The King also showed no signs of tiring of Fynn's song. Quite the contrary; he enjoyed it more and more with each visit. He did not tell Fynn that he must stay there forever, he simply ordered him to come again 'soon'. How many more 'soons' would Fynn be expected to stay for? He had no idea; he must talk to Lily about the matter.

When he asked Lily about his staying or going, she smiled sweetly at him and spoke to him as if he were a very small child who could not understand the simplest of things.

"The King will have you stay. He expects you to keep visiting him until you or he or both of you, dies. He cannot request you to come each day for the next so many days or years because he has no idea of time.

23

Nor does he want to mention death, his or yours, so he simply repeats the order 'soon'."

Fynn was shocked at the answer, even though he had feared it might be coming.

"What if I choose not to stay for many more 'soons'?" he enquired again, fearing the worst.

Lily laughed a little laugh and smiled lovingly at Fynn, a little understanding smile.

"You do not have a choice," she said. "The King has ordered you to stay here. He is delighted with your singing; you have brought him rest at last. He will never find it again should you leave. He is a King – do not forget – and what he desires he will surely have."

As she spoke, she saw that Fynn looked troubled; she must try to reassure him. What the King wanted was surely the best for Fynn?

"You will be well looked after. You can live here with us or in greater luxury within the King's own quarters. The King looks upon you as the greatest singer who has ever lived. You could have servants if you wish and the finest food and drink in the city. You will not need to work; your work can be your singing." -

Still Lily saw that Fynn's face had not changed; he was clearly unhappy. She tried again.

"What I say next will be of special interest to you. I have made the King aware of your desires. He knows that you would dearly love to perform to audiences who might love what they hear. He is in no doubt that the people of this city would, without exception, appreciate the gift of your voice. So far, you have sung to the King alone. He has it in mind that you should sing to the city! Now that he is certain of your talent, he is prepared to let you sing again and again to his very own people. To mark his decision, he will be asking you to sing a special song to the entire city."

Now she could see that Fynn was clearly excited.

"When shall I sing to the entire city?" he asked.

"Soon!" came the obvious reply.

When Fynn next sang to the King, the King asked him that very question.

"Would you like to sing to the entire city soon?"

Of course Fynn did not bother to answer. The tone the King used made it an order rather than a question. Fynn remembered he must not ask the King what 'soon' meant. However, he must have some idea of when he would be expected to perform. He could ask one question only.

"Is 'soon' before or after the next occasion on which I sing to your Majesty?"

"Before," came the briefest of replies.

Then that was it! Fynn had a 'day' or one 'soon' to prepare himself for the challenge.

# V

What a challenge it would be! What a magnificent occasion! Fynn went straight back to his room to prepare his voice and his songs.

He considered the task that lay before him. This would be the greatest mountain he had ever had to climb. All his life's achievements seemed very small alongside it. Imagine the thrill of it all: performing to a city full of strangers – a far cry from a hundred or so elves who knew him so well and took him for granted.

He must sing to the best of his ability. In front of such an audience, second best would simply not do.

Yet lately, Fynn feared, that was exactly what his singing had been – second rate. The King had not noticed the fall in standards but Fynn could not and would not, fool himse

His singing of late lacked the feeling he so desperately wanted. The sound would still have soothed the soul of any listener. However, Fynn knew something was missing. The special something that turned the listener to tears and made the heart miss a beat.

He must find it again in time for the event: but how? He had struggled and not found the answer ever since his arrival in this Kingdom. He had practised and practised his songs but still could not grasp the perfection he sought. Of equal concern was his inability to compose any new songs, try as hard as he might.

In his heart of hearts, Fynn knew the reason for this: it was the restlessness of the city that was to blame. Without peace and quiet, he could not refresh himself and fill himself with the spirit that was the key ingredient of his singing. He needed peace to produce his best – and he could find it nowhere.

He could not have tried harder to find peace. Fynn walked about the city, trying in the rhythm of his movement to find the pattern of some new song. However, everywhere he went he was met with the rush of inhabitants criss-crossing his path and interrupting any flow he sought.

Then he would try to find a quiet place within the walls. He sat under the shade of trees, basking alone in the warmth of some deserted square. However, others would join him, enquiring of his business. They came and went quickly but always buzzed about him like bees around honey. It occurred to Fynn that these people were nervous and had little left to work for in their lives. They would welcome any distraction such as himself.

In desperation, Fynn sought quiet in the sanctuary of the city library. There was a sign on the wall that read "SILENCE" but no-one took any notice; everyone talked to each other. When Fynn moved to a table in the corner, he found others joining him for no reason. Then those people would move on to another table and another. They could not keep still and, when seated for a few fleeting moments, showed the same nervous habits as the King himself.

Why not explore outside the city wall, Fynn asked himself. However, when he tried to pass through the city gates and beyond, he was immediately pounced upon by two agitated guards who told him that no-one could possibly leave the city without the King's special permission. Since Fynn did not have that permission, he could not leave the city.

Fynn had quizzed Lily on the matter.

"The guards were quite correct," she said.

"What about you then?" Fynn asked. "How did you manage to leave the city?"

"Every now and then the King will order one of the people from the city to venture into the great unknown. Their job is to check for the presence of any strangers. No-one ever finds anything of course but you must understand how nervous the King is. He fears attack from strangers at any time, though of course this will never happen. I was on such a venture when you found me, only I would rather pick flowers, I do not believe we have any enemies. We are too far from any Kingdom and no-one would want to conquer a Kingdom where there is no rest."

It was this last sentence of Lily's that Fynn remembered so clearly and it kept repeating itself in his troubled mind. Lily had been right – there was no rest in this city. Fynn had found that out for himself.

So, sitting in his room, Fynn could not contemplate spending the rest of his life here, a prisoner in a restless cell. The gift of his singing would mean less and less to him as he would sing the same old songs, gradually losing all feeling for them. This was not what he wanted. What use were the crowds if none of the pleasure was his?

He knew that eventually the King and his people would grow displeased with him as his singing lost its magic. Imagine the shame! They might release him then; but for how long would he have to suffer the worsening of his voice?

"I must go. I cannot stand this. I must find a way out for this city. I want to go home even if I must sing to myself alone for the rest of my days," Fynn whispered to himself with determination. It was a great thing to make up his mind to leave but how would he do it?

Fynn sat staring at the floor, his chin in his hands, trying to think up a solution to his problem. Suddenly he stood up and shouted, "Of course, of course, that's it!" He sat down again and began to work out the finer details of his plan. This is what he would do...

He would sing one song as usual to the King and his people. This would send them into a deep sleep - it had never failed to do so with the King. Then, instead of finishing after that song, he would pass immediately on to the next and then the next, without a pause between each. This would, he hoped, send the audience into an even deeper state of sleep. A sleep so deep that they would not wake when he had finished but stay asleep – hopefully for some time.

Whilst the King and his people slept, Fynn would run out of the city gates without any guards to stop him. He would then keep running to freedom, hoping that the sleep lasted or, if the people awoke, that no-one would bother giving chase.

There were risks of course. What if the sleep did not last and he were apprehended even before reaching the city gates? There was nothing Fynn could do about this; he could only hope. Then there was the problem with the continuous singing. Fynn would have to practise and practise more, drawing upon all his strengths to make the songs flow together, to breathe and keep singing. He must be inspired for this performance, as inspired as he was before he came to this Kingdom.

With these thoughts in mind, he began singing softly to himself, imagining he was back in the lands of Elfdom, amongst its beauty and peace. Slowly but surely, the words of the old songs came back to him. Their melodies made their way on to his tongue and the result was that pure sound he had once known.

Note followed note. Some were short, some long but always one after the other with never a gap between them. The songs were joined as one great offering. There was no time for new works but, by the time he heard Lily's familiar knock upon the door, Fynn was ready to sing. However, he could not have prepared himself for the sight that greeted him as he walked out into the street.

# VI

Huge crowds had assembled all around the magnificent square in the middle of the city. Fynn made his way, as a great guest of honour, between those who lined each side of the street. This city, normally so full of noise and hustle and bustle, was surprisingly quiet now. There was of course the sound of shuffling feet from the usual pacing, but most of those present managed to stay relatively still. However, there was not one, who was perfectly still, for each moved their limbs or face in the usual agitated manner. Each was looking forward to the first note and a little snooze.

A wooden stage had been hastily erected in the square and on it stood the King, a soft chair beside him, that he might enjoy the singing to the maximum. The people might doze standing, but not so their King.

As Fynn climbed the stage, he could see nothing but a mass of bodies hemmed in by the fine houses that flanked the square. It was a truly humbling experience – this many people wishing to hear him sing. This was a great honour but Fynn knew that this was the first time... and the last.

He waited for the King to introduce him and, without hesitation, this was exactly what the King did: in fewer words than most.

"This is Fynn. Sing, Fynn!"

That was it. Fynn must begin. He must not keep the King or his people waiting, he knew of their impatience.

As he sang, he saw the heads of the people droop as one and the King lowered himself to his seat. "So far so good," thought Fynn. Now he must continue to sing and not dare to stop. He did so, song after song, while the whole city dreamed. Soon the first sighs and whistle-breathing was heard. Then came light snoring and afterwards the thunderous snoring of those in a deep, deep sleep. Now was the time to move!

Fynn ran from the stage, his footsteps inaudible against the cacophony from the sleeping masses about him. Across the square he ran, down the main street and out through the city gates. He did not stop running until he felt unable to run any further. He walked briskly, half-ran then walked again, all the time creating a greater distance between himself and the city.

At last, Fynn came within sight of the stream where he had met Lily. Across that stream, maybe only a day's journey away, lay his homeland. Surely now he was safe?...

...Who knows how long it was before the sleeping city woke since time was not measured in that place. Let us say it was the best part of twenty-four Elfdom hours. When the slumber was finally broken, the crowd were alive with awesome energy, double their normal amount.

The King wasted no time. He realised what had

happened when he saw that Fynn had gone and heard the reports of a trail of elfin footprints heading out of the city. The King was furious.

"That elf is a traitor. He put us all to sleep so that this city might be left unguarded, ready for the enemy to attack!"

Pointing to a group of young men beside him, he said, "I see, with the growth of stubble on these faces, that we have been asleep for ages! What trickery… and to think that I trusted him and took him into my court! Well, he shall know the penalty for such a deed! Prepare the horses. We shall hunt him down and bring him back here to justice!"

Almost immediately, the King and his guardsmen were through the city gates. The speed of the horses was unimaginable. Driven on by their crazed riders, they covered the distance between themselves and Fynn in less than a quarter of the time it had taken the elf.

Thus, as Fynn neared the stream, he heard mad galloping behind him. He tried to run and hide but he had been seen; there was no chance of escape. They took him prisoner and rushed him back to the city.

Fynn, bewildered, could not believe the speed at which they travelled. He thought of how his singing had been his own downfall. The sleep had given them the energy to catch him when otherwise they may not have done so.

# VII

Fynn found himself in a prison cell. As the guard closed the door upon him, he mentioned in passing, "Soon you will be executed – King's orders."

That was it then. He, Fynn the singing elf, the famous singing elf, was to die for his troubles. How cruel a fate! He had not long to live. His ever so short life flashed before him. He saw his beautiful homeland, his family and friends. There was his mother singing to him and listening in turn to his song. Everywhere about him he saw trees, flowers, birds and wildlife of all kinds. Peace reigned amongst the wide-open spaces.

What must he do? There was no way of escape. Fynn began to cry.

Suddenly, there came the sound of a familiar knocking upon the cell door and Lily burst in, rushing over to him and hugging his small, elfin body.

"I am sorry Fynn. I have heard the news! Oh, it is so dreadful and it is all my fault, all my fault!" Lily wailed. "I brought you here to sing to the King. If you had not followed me then you would be safe among your friends. Oh Fynn, please forgive me even though I cannot forgive myself!"

Lily continued in a flood of words, "Soon you will die! I cannot possibly stand by and let that happen. I have a plan. Listen to me. We do not have much time."

Fynn wondered how might she save him.

"Before you die, the King must grant you one last request. That is written in our laws and it must be granted. You will ask to be allowed to sing once again. All the people of the city will be present. The King has ordered that all should witness the fate of the traitor elf. As you did before, you will bring sleep to everyone and escape again."

"This is a good plan," interrupted Fynn, "but will only result in the same agony – I shall be caught by the King and his men. I cannot run any faster and I cannot be sure they will sleep for any longer."

"You will not have to run," Lily was very excited now. "No, this time you will ride a horse."

"A horse?" Fynn was confused.

"Yes, a horse – one of the finest in the city. I will ride with you. We shall go together to the stream where we met and I shall return, leaving you there. You will be able to make your way to Elfdom before the King can catch you and I shall return to the city before the people awake. They will never know I have left the city in the first place."

"You are sure they would not catch me beyond the stream?" asked Fynn.

"The King and his men will venture no further. Darkness falls some short distance after; they are too afraid to risk the darkness."

"What about you, Lily? Won't you also fall asleep as I sing?"

"No, I have thought of everything. I shall slip away

and lose myself amongst the crowds. No-one will realise I have gone; their minds will be set on the awful spectacle to follow."

Lily continued, "I shall block my ears with these." She showed Fynn two perfectly shaped balls of soft silk. "See, I shall not hear your voice as I am hiding. I will make certain that I block out the tiniest trace of your sound. You must fetch me as soon as you have finished your singing. I will be waiting, wide-awake, in my own room."

Fynn sat staring for a moment, not quite able to understand all that he had heard.

"You are so clever, so brave, Lily," was all that he could say.

"Clever? Perhaps I am not *so* stupid; but brave? No, I am not brave. The plan cannot fail. The only possible risk lies with your singing. You must be able to repeat your last performance and send the audience into a deep and lasting sleep."

Fynn's expression changed. A look of determination swept over his face.

"I am singing for my life. You can be sure the singing will match any previous performance of mine. Indeed, I know this will be the greatest song of my life. The terror I have felt will be mixed with the indescribable relief of a last minute reprieve. Such a mix of emotions makes for the deep, strong surge of spirit that is the root of my song. My voice will be lifted to a higher plane. The audience and I will float above the ground. I know the effect; I have touched upon it for brief moments before this. For some seconds, soul will be separated from body. I know I can do this or perhaps I know my extraordinary situation will make me do this. The audience will sleep deeply, deeper than ever before. There is no need to prepare, no need to practise my songs."

Fynn had spoken. There was no doubting the power of his words, to which Lily listened in wonder. She began again, "Fynn, what you say sets my heart on fire, even more so your voice, should I hear it (which of course I will not), hidden away in my own house. Please Fynn," her voice took on an air of concern, "do not be angry with the King. He is old and set in his ways. He fears attack from every quarter. He sees danger when danger is not there. He is nervous, always on guard. He is to be pitied, not hated. You brought him the only peace he has known and yet it proved too much for him. It frightened him; to him rest and peace became potential enemies. He does not understand your mission; how could he? Your song belongs in a restful world, not in this restless Kingdom where there is no time to nurture and grow."

"I shall not be angry with the King or any of his people," said Fynn. "I shall be sad never to return to this land. Most of all it makes me sad to think of you, Lily, never able to rest, always busy. Surely you would want something more than this, for you seem to understand so much."

Lily looked straight at Fynn and smiled knowingly.

"This is my city. These are my people. This is where my family live and this is what I am used to. I have set my heart on wanting nothing more. I owe it to you, Fynn, to help you escape, but that is all."

At that moment, a guard barged through the door.

"It's time I was leaving," said Lily, winking at Fynn.

## VIII

The finest of chestnut mares was galloping at terrific speed towards the safety of Elfdom. Upon its back sat the triumphant Lily and Fynn. The escape had proceeded just as Lily had planned. Fynn had sung as never before, just as he said he would. The King and his people were asleep in an instant. Such was the beauty and sweetness of the song that they fell into a deeper dreamland more quickly than before. Fynn knew that this time they would stay asleep longer too.

When he had finished singing, he rushed to find

Lily and together they made their way through the tranquil city, leading the horse as they went. Once through the city gates, they mounted the horse and began the journey to freedom.

It did not take them long to reach the stream; at least it did not seem long to Fynn who remembered the time it took to walk that same distance.

"This is where I leave you," said Lily, climbing down from the mare. "You must find your own way from here."

Fynn stood silent. He did not know what to say.

"Good-bye then, Fynn," Lily shook his hand firmly.

"Shall we ever see each other again, Lily?" asked Fynn quietly.

"I think not. Our worlds are so different. You should return to the kingdom of elves where you can find true peace - with your wonderful voice, of course. I shall return home to all that I know and accept that for me there will never be peace. I must go now, Fynn, each second is a struggle for me. Good-bye!"

Lily turned, mounted and rode off towards the city. She did not once look back. Fynn continued to watch her until she became almost invisible. He was sad and yet happy at the same time.

Lily was right; there was no other way. It was the best for both of them. This was the end of his adventure in the Kingdom of light. He must cross over the stream, find darkness and then begin the long journey to Elfdom.

Carefully he picked himself a posy of the bright flowers; they would keep him company along the way.

# IX

It was the duty of all adventuring elves to report back immediately to the King of the Elves himself. An elf must tell his leader of all his experiences, good or bad. The wise King may then help the elf to understand the true nature of all that he has seen and heard on his journeys.

Fynn stood in front of the King of the Elves, who bade Fynn sit down and recall the details of his story. It was a long story. When Fynn had finished, the King of the Elves was silent and remained so for quite some minutes. During that time, he would look to Fynn, then to the ceiling and to the floor, in between time stroking his long grey beard. Fynn did not know what to make of all this but he knew he must be silent - he must not disturb the King's concentration.

At long last, the King asked him, "So Fynn, what do *you* think you have learnt from your journeying?"

Fynn replied. "I learnt that you cannot make songs without peace and rest, without simply stopping to sit and do nothing. The busy world, if it is too busy and does not ever allow rest, is no good for song. It does not nurture the spirit that makes the song. This I have learnt."

"I see," said the King, "and have you learnt any more?"

"Yes," said Fynn, "I learnt that it is the quality, depth and sweetness, the soul of my singing that matters most to me. To have an audience listen to my song is not as important as I once thought. If I had to choose between a better song sung to myself alone, and a very ordinary voice with which to perform to the largest of audiences, then I should choose the first. I must therefore always abide in a place where there is peace and rest even if those who live there grow accustomed to my singing and think it nothing very special. I am saying that Elfdom should be my home from now on."

"You show wisdom beyond your years, young elf. Tell me, and think hard now, what did you feel after all the events of this journey?"

Fynn answered him at once. It was clear he had given the matter a great deal of thought. "I found great joy in the friendship shown by Lily, joy at my escape from death and joy that I have all I need in this peaceful place. I have my song and I will learn to sing more sweetly. I cannot, I have discovered, ask for more.

"I felt sadness too," Fynn continued, "of course there was the sadness of leaving Lily but that had always seemed inevitable. Indeed, had my escape attempt worked the first time around, I would never have realised just how much she cared for me and how I fond I had become of her.

"No, there was a much greater sadness to feel – for the King and all his people. Even now, they will be busying themselves - never resting, always working their bodies, never at peace with themselves, never quiet, always noisy. I was able to break the spell that eternal daylight puts upon them, but not for long. Now I am gone and they shall never know any relief. I know that I cannot go back to the city to sing to all the people, for they would turn on me again. Besides, what could I do for them? I could not dwell with them as they would wish and what point is there in only singing one song or two? These people need the type of rest brought on by darkness, a lasting rest, not a minute or two of dreaming. Though there is nothing I can do for them, I fell as though I have deserted the King and his people."

Fynn finished. He had said enough; there was no more. He did not want to answer any more questions. The wise King of the Elves knew this and, although he said nothing for a moment, he still stroked his long grey beard.

"Very well then, Fynn," he said. "Come and see me tomorrow. We shall talk of plans for your future."

Fynn left the King, unsure of what the future might be. At the same time, the King was carefully plotting a future for the young elf. Before he could tell Fynn of his plans, there was a special something he must take from the elfin treasure chest.

Taking the golden keys from their place on the wall, he made his way downstairs to the secret vault of the Elf Palace. He unlocked two great doors, made his way through two rooms and unlocked the door of a third. With the fourth and largest key, he opened the treasure chest and took from it the item he needed. He smiled secretly to himself.

## X

The next day, Fynn came to see the King as arranged. The King of the Elves addressed him, looking very serious.

"We elves, Fynn, are naturally good servants of the kingdoms of this world. A good elf will believe this and take every opportunity to help others. Do you believe this, Fynn?"

Fynn nodded without hesitation. "I most certainly do," he said.

"Well then, Fynn, may I make a suggestion to you. It is a suggestion to which I have given a great deal of thought."

"Please tell me," said Fynn, excitedly.

"Fynn, I have here a very, *very* special cloak the like of which you have never seen before nor will ever see again. I see the look on your face: you think it is an ordinary cloak and do not see anything extraordinary about it, do you?"

Fynn shook his head, "No, begging your pardon, it appears to be an ordinary woollen cloak, a black one."

"Yes, Fynn," the King began again. "It appears as a simple black cloak but this cloak has a quite magical quality. Fynn, wearing this cloak, you can bring darkness to the skies – the same black as that of the cloak. Once the sky is dark, you may sing the sun to sleep with your song so that it sinks below the horizon. The moon, seeing the sky is empty of the sun and black in colour, will rise.

"Fynn, if you wish, you may take this cloak and bring night to the Kingdom of eternal day. You have an opportunity to save this restless people. You alone hold the key to their freedom. You alone have the voice to coax the sun from the sky. You alone, Fynn... with the help of the black cloak of course. What do you say, Fynn? Will you help them?"

There was no need for him to answer. Fynn took the cloak from the King of the Elves.

## XI

So the kingdom that was the kingdom of eternal light, now knows both day and night. Although it seemed a little strange at first, the city's people and the King himself now sleep soundly every night. They wake rested and have lost their nervous habits. Life is much slower there now. There is peace at last.

Each night, sitting by the side of the stream where he first met Lily, Fynn dons the black cloak that brings darkness to the sky. His song sends the sun to sleep and helps the moon to rise. When he takes off the black cloak, the sky clears again, he stops his singing and the sun climbs in the sky whilst the moon fades and descends.

During the day, Fynn rests himself after the night's singing. He enjoys his sleep – it is a chance for him to dream and to renew his strength for the long night ahead.

Fynn has considered visiting the city but he has a job to do. He must serve the kingdom with his song.

What about his dream audience? Well, no-one could ask for two greater listeners than the sun and the moon.

# THE RABBIT WHO BECAME KING
## I

The King thought himself the happiest man alive. His beautiful wife had given birth to a handsome baby boy and each time the King looked at his son, he saw, in the deep blue of the eyes and in the slight curve of the small mouth, a reflection of his own queen.

Disaster struck only days later when the queen, complaining that she felt a little out of sorts, fell quickly into a terrible fever. Its hands grasped her tight and would not let her wrestle free. For a week she battled, determined not to give in. Although she fought bravely, she could not resist the grip that choked her and on the seventh day she was finished.

During that terrible struggle, she had pleaded with her husband again and again, as if she knew she would die.

"Please, please look after Carlos. Don't let him come to any harm will you? He is all we have; he is something of me, something that might remind me of you lest you should forget me when I am gone."

In vain, the King told his queen that he could not possibly forget her and that she would live to see their son grow up and recognise herself in him. Yes, he promised, he would always watch over her son and keep him from harm. The prince was their greatest treasure and must be guarded accordingly.

As a small boy, Carlos knew the security of his nurse. She was a wonderful lady who cared for him as if he were her own son, never letting him out of her sight.

At the same time the palace guards were never far away, following the little boy wherever he went. The King had made a promise and felt he must keep it, though he questioned himself again and again as to what harm could possibly befall the boy.

About the time that Carlos began his schooling, there came reports of strange goings-on in the countryside far beyond the palace and its grounds. An old witch was doing the rounds of the woodland cottages. She demanded to be given gifts of different sorts or she would turn the owner into some kind of beast. So far there had been no confirmation of the old hag carrying out her threat but, nevertheless, she had managed to strike considerable fear into the hearts of the kindly woodland folk. They had given her what she had demanded, but she kept coming back for more and causing a great deal of nuisance.

The King did not believe in the old lady's powers but could not ignore the wishes of his people. Something must be done to rid them of her threats. So he instructed the palace guard to ride out upon their fine horses, to track down the mischievous woman and drive her from the Kingdom. The King himself would ride with his guard to show his people how seriously he viewed any complaints.

Sure enough, the King and his men came upon the hag, stooped in the doorway of one of the woodmen's cottages. She was cursing and pouring forth foul language upon the little man and woman who lived there. She waved her fist and pointed accusingly at them with a horrible, long fingernail. Her black cloak and dirty, unkempt hair made her appearance even more threatening. On seeing her, the King quickly understood why the people wanted rid of her.

Addressing her from high upon his horse, the King commanded that she leave the woods and his Kingdom, never to return. Now, others may have slung her in jail and made her stay there for the rest of her days, but not this King, who was kind-hearted, understanding and forgiving.

The hag, instead of being grateful for his mercy, spat at him and whispered a terrible curse under her breath. She shouted ugly words to him as she was led away by the palace guard, escorted to the boundaries of the Kingdom and let loose, never to be seen again.

## II

The King thought nothing more of the hag and indeed she was not seen in the woods again, so the cottage folk slept soundly at night. However, as the years passed, the King began to have disturbing dreams of the hag and of how she would come back to the Kingdom some day to take revenge upon him and his people. The King told himself that these were only silly dreams and he should not take any notice of them, but the dreams became more frequent, the shape of the hag more distinct, her featureless face more eerie (for he had never seen it underneath the hood of her cloak). 'Still,' the King reassured himself, 'we are safe here; no-one can enter my Kingdom without being seen. A stranger would soon be spotted, for each knows every other in this land. Even if a stranger were to steal into the city then the palace guard would be there to tackle them.'

Of course, all this worry about the dreams and the threat of a stranger came to the King because of his love for Carlos and his promise never to let him come to harm of any kind. The King decided to double the number of guards protecting Carlos and give strict orders never to let him out of sight, not even for a single moment.

From time to time, the King would organise a special audience with his son. Carlos was now sixteen years old and must be taught how to follow in his father's footsteps; one day he would have to rule as King just as his father ruled now. On such occasions, the palace guard was excused from the King's company; the King sat alone with Carlos in the main hall.

Whilst they were speaking, they were interrupted by a loud knocking on the heavy door. A guardsman entered, apologising as he made his way to the King.

"What on earth is it?" asked the King. "I've told you, we must be left alone to discuss these matters; you had better have a good excuse for your intrusion."

"I'm sorry, your Majesty, I would never have dared enter but for the news I bring being of such importance to your Majesty."

The guardsman told the King that a young woman, a recent visitor to the Kingdom, had spotted an old hag going about the woodland terrorising the people, demanding gifts and threatening trickery.

"The visitor tells us that the people are too scared to complain again to your Majesty; instead they have sent the visitor along as a spokeswoman. She has requested to see you immediately, such is the grave concern of the people."

The King turned pale at the guardsman's words, that mention of the old hag coming back to haunt his Kingdom.

"Very well. I shall speak with her, and this time we shall find the hag and put this nasty business behind us once and for all."

The woman was brought in to see the King.

"Leave us alone. Close the door behind you," commanded the King.

She told him, in great detail, that which the guardsman had relayed. As she spoke, the King looked straight into her blue eyes, admiring her appearance: simple peasant clothes but a handsome face and the loveliest of flaxen hair. Her story was obviously true. How could such a beautiful creature tell untruths?

"So you see, your Majesty, the old witch could strike anytime and anywhere in your Kingdom. I have come here today to warn you of her presence."

As she spoke, she looked first to the King and then to Carlos, smiling a strange smile at each one, smirking.

Then, by magic, she was transformed before their very eyes and in her stead was the very same witch of whom she had spoken! The King and Carlos were aghast – their mouths wide open!

"I have come for revenge, oh King," she announced. "Not for me now, begging from woodcutters, oh no! I have spent the time in exile perfecting my evil spells and you, oh King, or rather *you*, oh prince, shall be the first to experience their sting."

In an instant, she was muttering the most terrible words. She cast a hand out towards the hapless Carlos and turned him into – a rabbit!

"Now, your Majesty, you will wish you had put me in prison. But I shall be gone for good from your Kingdom; you will not catch me, nor will you catch your son!"

The witch let out a most horrible shriek of laughter. The King sat shocked – petrified - as the witch ran for the door. Assuming her disguise once again, she let

herself out of the palace - but not before whistling to the rabbit to follow her.

Seconds later the King woke from his fright and ran to the door, shouting orders to the guards. It was too late, the witch and the rabbit had disappeared into the busy city.

## III

Desperate times called for desperate measures. Immediately the King ordered a ban on the killing of all rabbits inside the city and amongst the woods and fields that surrounded its walls. Guards were posted all along the city walls and every rabbit attempting an escape was to be captured and brought to the King.

Of course, no rabbit *could* escape – none could climb the walls, but the King was in no mood for logic. He decided his son was either taking shelter in the gardens of the city houses, or had already escaped into the countryside beyond. The situation was hopeless.

Now, the people of the Kingdom liked nothing more than to sit down to a meal of rabbit stew, but on hearing of the wondrous tale of the witch, they understood the King's wishes. Not only would they be missing their favourite meal but also find their crops would be nibbled by the rabbits, who could now roam in their gardens without fear.

'The sooner the King finds his son, the better,' they all said, but in the meantime they must all play their part in the plan.

The King called upon each family in his Kingdom to bring him a rabbit which best answered the following description: it must be tame, showing strong signs of affection towards people; it must be handsome and, wherever possible, have deep blue eyes and a slight curvature of a small mouth.

Each family obliged, and very soon more than a thousand rabbits had been brought to the palace. Each was housed in a special cage lined with soft hay and containing the most delicious choice of fresh rabbit vegetables available.

The King continued with his plan. First of all, he went to each cage and whispered, "Carlos! Carlos!" to the occupant. If the rabbit did not twitch an ear or look at him or both, then it could not possibly be his son. Thus, half of the rabbits were confirmed impostors. Next, the King ruled out those whose eyes were not blue enough, then those with large mouths or those whose mouths seemed perfectly straight. Out went the ugly rabbits until the King was satisfied that his son was indeed amongst the six rabbits that remained seated before him on the palace table.

The King released the rabbits from their cages. Three of them made straight away for the door, and three remained on the table. His son must be one of these three. Each of the three looked at him adoringly and moved to him to be petted.

"Now I know," said the King, "that Carlos is here… but there cannot be three of him."

"Which one are you?" The King begged to be

answered but all of them seemed to be saying, 'It is me father, I am Carlos, choose me!'

"I have come this far and now I can go no further – I shall delay choosing until I can find a reason to make a choice."

The King sat back on his throne, exhausted and covered in rabbits.

## IV

Days went by and the King sat pondering, day and night. It was one of the guards who brought relief from his torment. He told the King that a wise, kindly old wizard had entered the city that very day and had offered, in return for food and a bed, to help the King if he were able.

The old wizard was sent for immediately. The King explained about the witch, his son and the three rabbits.

"I can indeed help you, but my help may hurt you," said the wizard. "I can reverse the spell and turn a rabbit into your son."

"Please, please go on, go on! You have saved me! Please give me back my Carlos!" the King shouted in triumph.

"I'm afraid it is not that easy," the wizard went on. "I have the power for one spell and one spell only. If you choose the rabbit that *is* your son then all will be well, but…" here he paused.

"But… but *what*?" asked the King, suddenly alarmed.

"But if you choose the wrong rabbit, one that is not

your son, then I can help you no further. I will have used my one and only spell, and all three rabbits before you shall remain just as they appear now for evermore… even though one of the three is your son."

The King considered the wizard's words.

"Then I have one chance only and I must be absolutely sure of my choice?"

"That is so," answered the wizard.

The King paced the floor. He knew he could not be sure and if he was not sure, how could he take the risk?

The wizard looked at the King, feeling deeply sorry for him.

"There is another option. Perhaps you would like to consider it?"

The King looked at him hopefully.

"Tell me; I need to know," he said, "I need you to help me. You are wise, tell me the answer."

"I am not sure you will like the wisdom of my answer," replied the wizard.

"Please, it cannot be worse than the hopeless choice I face."

"Very well, King, you may if you wish, choose the rabbit which you think is your son. You can call him Carlos, believe he is Carlos, treat him as a prince and crown him King when the time comes. You can never be absolutely sure, of course… but you can believe."

"If, on the other hand, you choose wrongly, then you will know for sure that the rabbit is not your son. You will doubt your own judgement and wonder which one, if any, of the two remaining rabbits is he. You will always be afraid that Carlos is lost forever."

"So you suggest that I trust and believe?"

"I suggest nothing, King, but I do not want to see you suffer any more than you have suffered thus far."

The King looked at the wizard, then towards the rabbits, and back again to the old man.

"I have made my choice," the King declared. "I believe this one is my son Carlos. I shall crown him prince and ask that the people understand just who he is."

The old man nodded wisely. "I think you have made the only decision you could make and, if I may say so, I think it is the right one."

## V

Following the King's announcement, the people of his Kingdom were rejoicing. Not only did they share their ruler's joy in finding their lost prince, but they were once again able to enjoy eating their favourite delicacy. Since Prince Carlos had, without a doubt, been rescued, there was no point in allowing the rabbit population to further explode. Crops and garden vegetables were safe once more.

So firm was the King in his belief that he ordered the two remaining rabbits in the palace to be set free in the woods outside the city.

"I must not hide my belief, I must show the strength of my decision," the King told his advisors. "I will not be afraid of the people: they must see the truth for themselves."

So the King organised a special ceremony to welcome back his lost son. All the people were to attend the event. It was to be a time of great rejoicing.

Crowds lined the streets, leaving a path for Carlos to hop down. Carlos, released from his cage some time ago, had grown used to the company of people and showed no fear in their presence. He appeared to positively enjoy weaving his way between legs, being picked up, sharing cuddles, paw shakes and bunny kisses with his future subjects. Carlos the rabbit was surely of the same temperament as Carlos the boy – kind, loving and well… human!

The King should never have feared the reaction of the people. They accepted Carlos without question, practising their bowing before him.

Carlos reserved the greatest show of affection for his father – clinging to him, front paws around the King's neck and his head on the King's shoulder. The King turned to look at his son and, in the bright sunlight of that day, knew for certain… the blue eyes he gazed upon sparkled like those of his long-lost queen.

# THE KING AND THE TOAD
## I

A lady toad was relaxing at the bottom of a deep, dark pond in a deep, dark wood. She was disturbed by a sudden shaking of the ground that made her pond shake so much, that the water splashed up and spilled over its muddy banks.

"What on earth is that?" she exclaimed, in a loud bubble.

The shaking and slopping did not go away. She decided to swim up to the surface to see what was causing such a disturbance.

Popping her eyes above the water, she saw a truly amazing spectacle. There were toads, thousands of them, marching in a great long line past her pond. She looked in both directions – a convoy of toads as far as the toad-eye could see.

Intrigued, she jumped on to the bank and, pulling one of the toads out of line, asked him what was going on.

"Haven't you heard?" asked the gentleman toad. "You'd better join the line. King's orders – we're all off to the palace!"

The lady toad decided that the gentleman toad was mad and wanted nothing to do with him or the rest of those marching lunatics.

"I'm off!" she said. "Have a nice time at the palace," she added sarcastically.

"I wouldn't jump back into that pond if I were you; they'll be out looking for you."

"Who? Who will be looking for me?" the lady toad asked, bewildered by his words.

"The palace guards – orders to search every pond and round up every toad in the land. Take it from me, it's best you come now or they'll take you by force."

The gentleman toad saw that the lady toad was still confused. "Listen, perhaps you haven't understood me yet. Let me explain a little further…"

He told her about the King's decree - every toad in the land was to come to the palace. Each would be treated very well and given the best worms and flies as a thank-you for making the journey. Each toad in turn would receive a single kiss from the King. The kissing would continue until one of the toads turned into a princess. The rest of the toads would then return to their ponds.

To the lady toad, this all sounded a little ludicrous. Still, what harm could there be in such an exercise? If this crazy King wished to kiss thousands of toads, why should she be concerned? It was an inconvenience to her but, she considered, a night or two dining out at the palace would be really rather exciting and perhaps she could do with a little adventure.

She joined the line and, as she hopped on her way to the palace, she wondered how it was that important people like princes and kings had nothing better to do with their spare time…

Meanwhile, the King sat upon his throne preparing himself for the kissing marathon. The toads were to be housed in special tanks in all the rooms of the great palace. Each room was positively bulging at the seams with toads. He was not looking forward to his work. Was he mad or was there a genuine reason for his scheme?

Five years ago exactly to this day, the King was quite happy in the company of his beautiful princess. He was a prince in those days, his father still being King. On that fateful day, his beautiful princess was turned into a common toad.

It was his father's fault. The former King became involved in a terribly heated argument with a quick-tempered witch. The witch, hysterical, took it out on the King's daughter-in-law. Incidentally, the witch later apologised but by then it was too late: the princess had left quickly for a pond. The witch felt so sorry about what she had done that she gave up being a witch and so couldn't reverse the spell even if the toad could be found.

The situation remained thus for these five years during which time the old King passed away. The prince, now the new King, remembered something his nanny had told him in a fairy tale – he decided that if he kissed the princess-toad he would restore her to her former glory and she would now become queen.

However, even if the fairy tale were true, the King would still have to find the toad. He could waste an awful lot of time messing about looking in the woods and ponds. He could not be sure that he was not kissing the same toad over and over again. He needed a practical solution to the problem. He, the King, would not go to the toads; the toads would come to him.

Now, the new King was a very handsome man. After the princess was turned into a toad, a lot of ladies became very interested in marrying him. There was one beautiful girl who, to this day, was very interested in becoming the new queen. However, the young King was an honourable man. He would not marry again until he was absolutely sure that the princess had disappeared forever. This was why he had decided that he must round up all the toads in the land, and kiss them. If none of the toads turned into a princess then he would marry the other lady, whose name was Annabella.

Now, the King had never kissed a toad before – he much preferred kissing beautiful ladies. Each toad was to be taken from its tank and rinsed in pure spring water mixed with the sweetest smelling herbs from the forest. Then, and only then, would the King give the creature a kiss. It was not a proper kiss, more a little peck on the back of the head.

The King kissed quickly. No toad turned into a princess and the King was sad because he could not find his missing wife. However, he was very glad when there were only a few hundred toads left to kiss. Soon there were only one hundred and then the King was left with the last ten toads to kiss.

Our lady toad was amongst this group. She had waited patiently for her turn and was pleased to find herself next in the queue. In moments, everything would be over and done with and she could be out of the palace on the way back to her pond.

The lady toad was plucked from the tank and rinsed in the sweet smelling water.

"Yuk!" she thought to herself, "What are they trying to do to me?"

She sat in the hand of one of the King's servants, staring straight ahead, waiting to be put back into the tank again.

Suddenly, she felt as if she had exploded! A peck on her back and she was transformed. She had grown indeed – she was the beautiful princess!

# II

The King and the princess stood together, speechless. He saw that she was just as beautiful as ever. He smiled at her and took her hand, but she looked shocked.

"What has happened to me?" she exclaimed. "I was a toad, what am I now?"

"You are what you were," answered the King quietly, trying to calm her.

"What I was?" she cried alarmingly.

Then the King had to explain, as quickly and as gently as possible. After all, this kind of thing just didn't happen to you every day. No wonder the princess was in a state of shock.

As he told her the story, the princess relaxed just a little but she was terribly upset – like a toad out of water! When he had finished his explanation, she turned to him and said, "I am sorry but I have no memory of my life as a princess. I have been a toad for as long as I can remember, which isn't very long – a toad only remembers things for a day or two."

All that night, the King tried to comfort her. He told her, as she had told him, that she would soon forget about every having been a toad; it would only take a day or two.

"But," she argued, "that is the case only if you are turned from a princess into a toad – you forget in a day or two. What happens when you change back from a toad into a princess? Perhaps I will never forget my toad days as I now have the memory of a princess!"

The King had no answer to this but said honestly, "We must hope, it is true, but I feel sure that you will forget... and soon; then you will live your life as a beautiful queen – my wife!"

He tried very hard to encourage her, to make her happy.

"Tomorrow," he said, "I have organised a special occasion in your honour. Tomorrow will be a wonderful celebration when you are crowned as my queen before all the people of this land. Yesterday a toad, today a princess, tomorrow a queen – imagine!"

The princess burst into tears at his words.

"I think perhaps," she sniffed, "I think I should go to bed now. I'm sure I will feel much better in the morning."

On hearing her words, the King's spirit lifted. It would take time, a little time he hoped, but thanks to the miracle of the kiss, everything would be as normal very soon.

The princess did not sleep at all well that night. She dreamt over and over of her coronation – she was about to receive her crown when someone in the watching crowd would point out that she was not the queen but a slimy brown toad. Then the rest of the people would realise what she was and run away in disgust. She would be left heart-broken and the King, in dismay, would leave her too. Everyone would disown her.

Then she dreamt that she found herself as a princess, swimming in a nearby pond. She would like to talk to the toads in the pond and join in their toad games but they would mock her with croaky laughs and tell her to leave the pond. She would argue with them and say that she did not want to leave. They would tell her that she was silly and did not belong there.

When the princess awoke, she was faced with the awful truth: she still thought and felt like a toad but looked like a princess. She did not want to be a princess. For her the pond was her natural home, not the rich corridors of this lofty palace.

She did not belong on land: the air was dry, the food strange. To stand was awkward, to swim was natural, or to hop. She longed for a tasty morsel of some insect or slug.

The princess sat up in bed. She shook herself.

"No," she announced, "I must be strong. I am a princess and not a toad. This must be my home and everything in it, everything that has nothing to do with being a toad. The memory will pass; the memory *must* pass. I was born a princess; I must learn to be a princess once more!"

The princess went to find her husband.

"Good morning," she said with a sunny smile on her face. She put her arms about him and, turning him around, kissed him on the back of the neck.

# III

The princess looked more beautiful than ever in her dress of white silk. She was indeed ready to be crowned as queen.

The King sat with her as they waited in the palace. Outside the final preparations were being made for the great ceremony. The King looked at her adoringly – how things had a way of working themselves out! He could not believe the change in her. She was composed, behaving as though nothing of consequence had happened yesterday. He could scarcely believe his good fortune.

There came a knocking at the door. A servant entered.

"Please, your Majesty, the Lady Annabella wishes to speak with you."

The King had been dreading this moment. Still, he considered, it was better dealt with now. He could rid himself of this awkward matter and enjoy the coronation to come.

"Let her in, please," the King replied.

Annabella strode into the room. She was not alone: an older lady was with her.

"Your Majesty," she began, "we have come to see you and the princess to convey our very best wishes to both of you."

There was something strange about the tone she used. She seemed to be sneering at the King.

"Why, thank you," replied the King. "It is gracious

of you to be so thoughtful."

At his words, Annabella erupted in a fit of fury.

"Gracious? Good gracious! What are you doing, oh fine King? You would marry a toad, would you? You would keep me waiting and not take me as your bride but instead take a toad! Well then, if it is a toad you love, let us turn *you* into a toad!"

Turning she called, "Mother!"

At her command, the older woman stepped forward and with one wave of her cruel hand, turned the hapless King into a croaking toad.

The princess shrieked. "What have you done? What have you done?"

"I have done exactly as you and the King did to me; I have broken your heart. Now be quiet or my mother, evil witch that she is, will likewise turn you back into a toad!"

"No, never!" cried the princess.

"Be quiet or I will have you as a toad!"

"Never, never, you will..."

In a blinding flash of light, the witch turned the screaming princess into a toad.

Now there could be no coronation. Instead, two very ordinary-looking toads left the palace and made for the ponds in the woods.

## IV

The princess-toad and the King-toad made straight for the same old pond in which the princess-toad used to live.

Now it was the King-toad's turn to be shocked and sad. What a terrible fall: from a mighty King to a lowly toad! He would never see his palace again, only the brown of this muddy water. He had lost his servants, his people and his dignity. He could not help himself; he was so depressed. He fell to the bottom of the pond and sat there motionless – like a stick-in-the-mud.

The princess-toad on the other hand, felt she was back in her rightful home and in her rightful state. She had deliberately forced the hand of the witch. She wanted to be turned back into a toad and, of course, she wanted to spend the rest of her life with her husband the King-toad.

It was her turn to comfort him now. She dived down to the bottom of the pond to speak to him.

"I know," she began very softly, "that being a toad is not what you expected or wanted. People think a toad's life is dull and hard. They find us unattractive and would never understand why a person should choose to become a toad. At the moment you cannot understand but please let me explain some of the good parts of the toad life."

"You will have to try very hard to persuade me that being a toad is nothing more than a being a miserable failure," the King-toad said sulkily.

The princess-toad was not at all upset by his tone.

"Listen carefully," she said. "When you were a

King, you were watched every moment of the day. Your manners had to remain impeccable; every word that you uttered could be overheard and used against you. You could never really say what you thought. You had enormous responsibilities looking after all those citizens. You might be called upon to fight another kingdom.

"Then there were the day-to-day duties: banquets to attend, foreign visitors to talk to, buildings to open, schools to visit, places to be "seen" in.

"As a toad, you have none of these worries. Yours is a simple life. You can do exactly as you please. You can say what you want, make friends with who you want, go wherever you like."

The King-toad was listening carefully; perhaps things weren't so bad after all.

"Rest a-while. Things always appear brighter after sleep."

The King-toad felt a bit better but still not quite right – but what did it matter? Sleep or no sleep, he would forget about being a King very soon. In fact, he would remember only as long as his memory allowed him, which as we already know, is only a day or two…

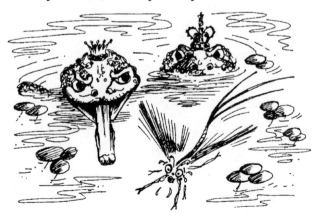

# MASTER OAK

## I

Peter had never been this way before. He considered himself something of an explorer. It had taken him three or four hours of fast walking to reach the woods. He had always wanted to come here; there

seemed something special about the place when he viewed it from the distance of his own home. He wanted to come here alone, to concentrate his thoughts on the wood itself. Having company was fine but always a distraction.

As Peter approached the edge of the woodland, he felt a tingle of excitement run through him. He imagined what might lie in store. As soon as he entered the wood, he realised that his imagination had been far too small.

Gazing up into the canopy of the towering oak and beech, he felt himself shrinking. He lost himself in the great mass of brown and green stretching above him. Tilting his head back to see further and further up to the tops of the trees, he felt dizzy. He filled his mind with the beauty of it all: the jigsaw of the blue sky and verdant leaf. How happy, how content he felt!

Scared that he might lose himself completely and topple over, Peter lowered his head; the spinning sensation ceased and the world stood still once more.

On through the wood he marched. The trees seemed to shuffle closer together, joining branch arms and twig hands, snuffing out most of the daylight. Peter thought this most wonderful. It became a secret, darker place; a place for trees and not for sky. Here, under the continuous umbrella of the giant trees, Peter felt safe and secure. This was a den for him, a place to come to again and again. The wood where he stood, like a statue gazing, was his resting place.

Peter felt he must explore a little further. It was so good to fix your gaze and heart upon what lay before you but there may be other exciting treasures yet to discover. Further and further into the wood he travelled until he was sure that he had reached the very heart of it. It seemed like nightfall to him, so thick was growth of the trees.

Once again, Peter stopped in his tracks and breathed in the woodland air. He closed his eyes and listened. He heard a voice!

"Stop your dreaming. Come and talk to me."

Then again, "I'm here behind you. Come, don't

ignore me."

Peter was not dreaming. Twice the soft voice had spoken. It was not an unfriendly tone, rather the opposite – calm and inviting. It was a man's voice and the words were slow and deliberate.

Peter spun around. He saw – nothing! Perhaps the man was hiding or had run off as soon as he saw Peter turn. Then he heard the voice again.

"I'm here, right in front of you. Walk straight forward and you will bump into my trunk. Mind my roots as you come closer. It is very painful to have someone step on your roots!"

Peter realised it was a great oak tree speaking to him. This indeed was a magical place where even the trees could talk! He walked forward a few paces, carefully avoiding the twisted roots of this huge tree.

Peter wanted to show the tree that he was a friendly sort and so introduced himself in a very humble tone.

"Hello, Master Oak, my name is Peter. I am very pleased to meet you. I must say that I am charmed by the wood in which you live. It is a paradise. It possesses a beauty unlike any other place I have ever visited. In this wood, I feel so different, so free. I have no cares when looking at the blue of the sky and the green of the leaves. I am tiny next to you and all the other great trees of the forest. I like to feel tiny, it makes me realise how big the world really is and how much I have yet to discover."

Peter continued. He wanted to tell Master Oak

just how wonderful Master Oak and his wood were.

"I look at you, Master Oak, and I marvel at your appearance. You are so very tall and proud. You are naturally handsome and strong. You are old and wise and know all the secrets of the wood. I should like to learn from the trees of this wood and now I have found you, Master Oak, and you speak so that I can understand… Oh Master Oak, you don't know how wonderful I am feeling! But please Master Oak, perhaps I am talking too much. Forgive me, I am so excited. Please tell me about yourself."

"I will do so," said Master Oak, "but first let me say what an equal pleasure it is to meet you. How polite you are! You show such great understanding of my home and yet you are so young. I know that you too will grow to be mighty of mind, wise and strong of heart. In tree language, you would be known as a fine specimen of a sapling. But Peter, you seem surprised to be able to speak with me and yet there are thousands of trees in this forest. Did you never converse with them?"

"No, never," replied Peter. "They have never spoken as you yourself have spoken."

"Then you must listen for their voices," said Master Oak, "Let us be quiet for a few moments and listen together."

Peter stood in front of Master Oak and waited and waited but he heard not one single word he could recognise.

"There! You hear it?" asked Master Oak.

"I hear nothing except for the rustling of leaves and the creaking of branches in the breeze. I do not hear the kind of words you are sharing with me," Peter remarked.

"I am puzzled," said Master Oak. "I hear their language loud and clear. I understand what they are saying to me. Yet, you say you hear no words."

"I do not," replied Peter.

"It is as she said it would be then," said Master Oak thoughtfully.

"Who? What did she say?" enquired Peter.

"It was a long, long time ago when I was but a short stick, half as tall as yourself. There were few leaves upon my short, stubby branches. A young girl came stepping through these very woods and came to a stop by my side. She spoke to me in her own language, the same as yours, and immediately I understood her and could reply using the same.

"The girl, named Rosa, told me that I was a very, very special tree. I had been given a secret gift but she would not tell me what that gift was. 'None of the other trees possessed this gift,' she added.

"I learned that it was Rosa who had planted the acorn from which I grew. The fairies had given her the seed, telling her about the magic contained within it. I saw Rosa this one time only. She told me she was moving away with her family to another land. She told me I would grow into a mighty oak tree; the

fairies had given her their promise. Then, just as she was leaving, she told me one final secret. I remember her words as clearly as they were said yesterday – 'when you are old and wise, you will have the power to save this woodland where you live... and others like it!'"

For a moment, Master Oak was silent. When he next spoke, it was with a notable sense of urgency.

"I realise everything now!" he exclaimed. "Peter, you must go back to your home and tell your King all about our meeting – but no-one else must hear! Then bring the King alone to see me; just the two of you. I must speak with him. Ask me no questions now, Peter. Please do just as I say."

## II

Peter stood before the King, explaining all that had happened in the wood. Now, the King was a warm-hearted and kind man. He did not scoff at Peter's words as others may have done. Besides, he knew of Peter and his family and knew they would not tell lies.

The King agreed to pay a visit to Master Oak. Peter led the way, this time on horseback. He was impatient to reach his destination. Indeed, they set out from the palace within minutes of Peter's arrival: the King could see just how eager the boy was.

Peter carefully retraced his steps through the wood. The two of them walked, leaving their horses tethered at the edge of the trees. It did not take long for Peter and the King to reach Master Oak.

"Your Majesty," began Master Oak, "you do not know me nor I you - except I recall the one occasion you rode through these woods on a small pony. You were with your father; you were such a small boy! Since then I have not seen anyone from the palace."

There was a slight pause before the great tree resumed.

"King," he started rather solemnly, "I do not know what kind of man you are. I would hope that you are a person of integrity and good-heartedness for the matter on which I am about to speak is a serious one that requires your careful and sympathetic consideration."

"Master Oak," interrupted Peter excitedly but with as much politeness as possible, "I can speak for the good nature of our King. He is a truly kind man who listens carefully to the problems of others and would help wherever possible."

"Thank you, Peter, for speaking on behalf of your King. As I have already met you and trust your nature and your word, then I must assume that your King is indeed a helpful, kind and considerate person."

"King," began Master Oak once more, "I need your help. Of late, I have heard strong rumours. There has been a terrible whispering amongst the trees; there has been much rustling of leaves and waving of branches. The word is, oh King, that the wood itself will not last much longer. The great trees, such as myself, will be cut down just as has happened in other woods not far from this one. We know of this – the trees speak to each other and tell the awful truth of the events.

"Can you, your Majesty, put my mind at rest? Can you promise that this wood will remain as it is, at least in your lifetime? Can you assure me that none of the trees around me, nor I, will be cut to the ground?"

The King had no hesitation in answering.

"Mighty Master Oak, I will never allow you or your fellow trees to be cut to the ground either in my lifetime or forever more. Now that I know your concerns, I will pass a law that prevents such action. The law will last forever. Peter has explained the magic of this wood to me and now I have experienced that magic for myself. It has a wondrous atmosphere and is a heavenly haven that must never be destroyed. Furthermore, your own existence will remain a secret known only to Peter and myself. If my people knew about you, they would be here in their thousands and would spoil the very wonder of that which they had come to see."

"I am overjoyed to hear your words but the word from the other woodlands is that many trees are being killed as we speak. They are cut down for crops to be planted or houses to be built. The people in this Kingdom are lucky to have a King such as you. However, some of them are becoming greedy; they want a bigger house or sometimes more than one house. If they grow more crops than they need, they can sell them to make more money – money that they do not need. The people want more and more and more of everything. They will not be content until they have chopped down every tree in every wood in this Kingdom. Some of them may make excuses saying they must have wood for fire but they already have plenty of wood with reserves to last them for years to come.

"King, these people have no hearts. If they did, they would not destroy such beauty. What is the point of having more wealth if they throw away the greatest riches on earth? Once we trees are gone, we are gone forever; no-one has the patience to re-plant and watch us grow again. Please, your Majesty, can you… will you help us?"

There was an air of desperation in Master Oak's voice. It was not long before the King answered. His tone was sound and sure. He meant what he said.

"Master Oak, I am very sad at your words. I did not know of the events of which you speak. I cannot but trust the people of this Kingdom because that is in my very nature. Now I hear that there are those whom I cannot trust. I have left them to their own devices and this is what has happened. From now on, they shall be watched more closely to make sure that they obey the laws.

"The laws themselves shall be changed to protect not just this woodland but every wood in the Kingdom. It shall be considered a serious crime to damage the trees. Only when it is absolutely necessary for trees to be cut for firewood shall felling be allowed. I give you my solemn word, Master Oak, from now on you shall hear good news from your fellow trees, not bad."

The King, Peter and Master Oak exchanged "good-byes". The King was keen to rush back to the palace as fast as he could to make the laws of which he had spoken. Peter promised Master Oak that he would be back. Master Oak thanked the King and said he would be delighted to share Peter's company again.

### III

Every weekend without fail, Peter would visit Master Oak. Throughout the year he kept up his journeys to the wood, noticing the passing of the seasons: summer to autumn, winter to spring, back again to summer.

Master Oak had told him of the timeless habit of shedding his leaves, of how the winter seemed so cold when a tree lost its layer of green clothing. He told Peter that spring was his favourite season.

"The days become longer, all my favourite animal friends come out to play and there is plenty to do, what with all those leaves to grow back. All the trees are talking again; there is sap rising in the tree trunks; it is a busy time, very exciting. Winter, on the other hand, is a very slow time. Not much happens, nothing much to talk about: all the animals have hidden away, most of the birds have migrated – all is quiet."

"Do you not you like the peace of winter when you can have a rest from all that growing?" Peter asked Master Oak.

"You have a point there, Peter. Yes, I suppose I do – but I still much prefer spring and summer. I like the action, yes that is what it is, the action."

Peter asked Master Oak about the news from the other trees.

"Ah Peter, it is as your King said it would be. There is nothing but good news to report. The axes have stopped swinging in the woods. There is no more cutting down of trees. Peace is being restored to the woods. Tree trunks left on the ground after the felling have been taken away: no-one wants those dead bodies hanging around as a reminder of the terrible deeds.

"Animals are coming back into the forest – they were scared away by the chopping and sawing and the loud voices of the woodcutters. Tiny trees are appearing in the gaps and these will grow quickly as they have the light around them. The bigger trees have begun to recover from the shock and are now talking amongst themselves. They are able to plan for future seasons knowing they are safe. I have told them of your King, they know of his plans. There is nothing now to destroy the peace and magic of our wonderful woods."

One summer night, Peter lay in bed unable to sleep.

The air was hot and sticky. The sun had shone in the morning but by afternoon the clouds had moved in; they were white and wispy at first, changing to grey and fluffy until now when they filled the sky, almost black, and angry. Peter could not settle. He looked out at the sky.

"There may be a storm," he said to himself. Then he thought again. "No, the storm never comes. You want it to but it never does. Instead, the heavy sky sits on you and waits until a wind eventually blows the cloud away. No, the storm never breaks to bring relief, not when you desperately need it to."

"It's no use. I can't sleep!" Peter muttered under his breath. "Let's read instead." He could not settle to his book either so he sat up in bed to think for a while.

A thought flashed across his mind.

"That is it! That is what I shall do!" he whispered loudly to himself. "Better to have an adventure and go to sleep a little later than waste all this time trying to sleep in the first place."

Peter slipped out of the house – no-one would notice his leaving and he didn't want to spoil his adventure by explaining his plans. He led one of the horses from the little stable and, once clear of the yard, jumped on to her back.

The horse looked a little confused. Where might she be going on a hot summer's evening with a storm coming soon? She must simply follow her master's orders and hope that he knew what he was doing.

Peter reasoned to himself that there was enough daylight to reach the wood, spend some time in conversation with Master Oak and return home before nightfall. This was so exciting, why had he never done it before? Indeed, he was so excited that he did not notice the sky gradually darkening further.

The first he knew of the storm was a thin flicker of light across the sky somewhere in the distance, followed by an equally distant rumble of thunder. Nothing to worry about; the storm always threatens but it never arrives, never. His horse knew differently. She could smell the approaching rain on the wind and she did not like it. She tried to tell Peter, shaking her head slowly at first and then rapidly with more force and urgency.

"Come on girl, nothing to worry about," Peter said to the horse reassuringly. "Nearly there, nearly there."

However, the lightning and thunder were coming closer by the minute and the first drops of rain were beginning to fall. Peter was less confident now but he could not turn back and give up on his adventure.

They were within sight of the edge of the wood when the storm moved directly overhead: the rain fell in torrents; thunder crashed about them; lightning set the sky alight. The horse reared up, then stopped still. Peter planned to drag her to the edge of the wood and tether her under the shelter of the trees but she would not move. She could not tell him that she did not want

to be left standing under trees with the lightning splitting open the sky – she felt safer, if wetter, to stay out in the open.

Peter did not know what to do. Suddenly a great streak of lightning rent the sky from top to bottom. A terrible scream rang out, louder than any he had ever heard before. Then, the sound of moaning mixed with the clap of thunder. Peter had not had time to recover from the shock when he saw great plumes of smoke rising from the wood, followed by flames, huge tongues of fire licking the trees.

Immediately he let go of the horse and ran. He was terrified. The acrid smell of smoke filled his nostrils. He was soaked to the skin. Coming to a clearing just short of the middle of the wood, he stopped dead in his tracks. He had feared the worst. Something inside of him had told him all was not well. His instinct had not lied to him.

There before him amongst the flames, lay part of the trunk of a huge tree, split clean away from the remainder. The charred remains of other smaller trees and branches added to the bonfire.

In desperation, Peter called out, "Master Oak, Master Oak! Is that you? Answer me, Master Oak!" Peter already knew it was he and Master Oak did not answer his cries.

# IV

Peter and the King stood where the mighty Master Oak had once stood. The woodcutters had taken down the rest of the stump trunk. They had made a neat pile of logs from the trunk. The King had ordered that the logs must be taken to Peter's house. Peter could then decide what to do with them.

It was now a week after the storm and all the debris from that terrible night had been cleared away from the middle of the wood. The only clue as to what had happened there was the massive tree stump and the space around it where other trees had fallen prey to the fiery sky. No-one except for Peter and the King would ever know what marvellous giant had once lived there.

Peter turned to the King and said, "He was a great friend. It sounds ridiculous but, in the end, he became half person and half tree. I could talk to him and tell him things about my life; he would listen and give advice. He was so wise, he taught me so many things about the beauty, life - and death – of Nature. I shall miss him so. This wood will never be the same without him."

The King put his arm around Peter's shoulder.

"Yes, it is true. Master Oak has gone and he will be sorely missed. However, the mark he left lives on. Think of all the trees he has saved; think of the wonderful woods we still have as a result of his speaking to us. These woods will live on forever as a reminder of Master Oak. Think of the other children playing in all the other woods. Like you, they will find peace and tranquillity under those mighty trees. In his own way, Master Oak will be speaking to them every time they play in those woods."

There was silence between the two of them, nothing more to be said. They turned and made for the edge of the wood.

For the whole of autumn, Peter stayed away from the wood; nor did he wish to visit during the winter. The pile of logs sat as a constant reminder of Master Oak. What should he do with them?

One freezing night in January, when the howling wind blew through the house and the snow lay deep and solid upon the ground, Peter decided to burn some of the logs. He was alone in the house and would be able to see for himself when the magical old tree trunk burst into flame.

The kindling had caught nicely; now he would burn the logs. Peter took one of the smaller logs and placed it carefully in the middle of the burning kindling. Slowly, the log grew hotter and then suddenly burst into flame. Peter waited patiently. He saw nothing except a sea of orange, he heard nothing except the crackle and spit. He placed another log on the fire. Still nothing.

Then he took two more logs and then another and another until the fireplace could hold no more. He sat in his chair and waited, watched and listened. The fire grew hotter and hotter; the wood crackled and spat but there was nothing more. The flames reached higher and higher and then sank, degree by degree.

The wood, mostly burnt, glowed in the grate.

Peter shouted at the fire in desperation.

"Do something! Say something! You can speak, can't you? Tell me something, anything!"

The wood did not stir. There was not a sound from the grate.

Peter still stared straight ahead at the glowing embers. What had he expected? Did Master Oak not say that all the trees stopped their talking in winter; winter was a time for sleeping. Yet, Peter thought, the fire would give energy to the wood and the old trunk would come alive and …

It was hopeless. Master Oak was dead and that was that. What did it matter whether he burnt the logs in winter or summer? The logs were part of a dead tree; the sap of life had long ceased to flow through their veins. No amount of heat from fire could bring back life to the dead. Peter left the fire alone and turned towards his bed.

In the morning, he rose early. He took the cold

ashes from the grate and carefully wrapped them in some old sacking. He took the bundle under his arm and walked out into the icy cold morning air.

It was barely light in the world. Peter walked towards the edge of the yard and made his way slowly to a small copse of trees in the meadow beyond. There he unwrapped the sacking and, holding it aloft, allowed the strong wind to blow away the ashes of mighty Master Oak.

## V

It had been a long winter that year; spring was a long time in coming. Peter waited until the first warm April day and then set out on his journey to the wood. He came again to the spot where he had stood with the King that previous summer. He still felt sad; he could not help himself. What he expected or wanted to find there, he no longer knew. He simply had to go there.

The spot was not quite so bare now. New grasses were beginning to grow and the early spring flowers had taken the opportunity to invade the area. He saw one or two saplings poking their heads above the soil.

It was a long cycle. It was time for the new to replace the old. Nature was as simple and as complicated as that. But Peter did not want the new - he wanted the old. Without knowing why, he spoke out aloud.

"Master Oak, I see your withered stump. Are you

there Master Oak? Are you there? You can speak to me. It's Peter, your old friend, Peter!"

Silence. He expected it of course.

Peter tore himself away from the grave and made for another part of the wood, untouched by fire. Here, the trees grew as usual, their leaves beginning to unfurl from the spring buds.

He looked skywards as he had done the very first time he had visited the wood. He saw again the jigsaw of blue, green and brown. He relived that feeling of peace, of spirit rising like the sap in those spring trees.

He looked and listened, and listened more. He tried so very hard to hear the trees speaking words to him. There was nothing except for the rustling of tiny leaves and the cracking of finger twigs. The breeze blew harder; the rustling and cracking grew louder. Still it made no sense to him.

Peter stopped craning his neck and looked down again. It was true he had lost his friend, Master Oak, and he would never hear the trees speak, but he must continue to come here.

He felt sure that he would grow in wisdom enough to one day understand exactly what it was the trees were trying to tell him.

# THE TALE OF THE
# EVERLASTING CHOCOLATE CAKE
## I

There once was a very poor kingdom full of very poor people and a King who was really not much better off. However, because everyone was so poor and there were very few possessions to be had, there was very little to fight over. So, everyone got along very well. Jealousy and greed were unknown. Although the people were poor, no-one ever starved, for this Kingdom was renowned for its successful cultivation of wheat and its endless supplies of bread.

Bread, bread and more bread; it was the food of the Kingdom. Loaves were white, brown, wholemeal, granary or multigrain - but they always tasted of bread. The shape of the loaf was also very important: rolls, sticks, cobs, rings, plaits and buns – but each tasted of bread. After centuries of eating bread, the people could only look forward to centuries more of bread consumption.

Now, the King was very kind-hearted but, like his father before him and a string of fathers before his father, he was not a successful ruler. He did not seem to have the power to attract riches of any kind. As a consequence, he had nothing in the way of excitement to offer his people, not even something exciting to spread on their bread.

Imagine the King's excitement when he dreamt one night of a most delicious chocolate cake. Imagine his disappointment when he awoke the following morning to realise that the cake was not for real and instead for breakfast he would be dining on his usual – a loaf of bread. This, at least, was a special loaf of bread, having a crown emblem neatly embossed on the top of it.

"The cake was nearly mine," he complained to the queen. "I could almost touch it, smell it, taste it – and then it disappeared, gone forever!"

"Well dear," said the queen, trying to help her husband, "try dreaming again and again and then perhaps your dream will come true. If not, you'll have come a lot closer to a cake than the rest of this kingdom!"

She was right of course. Firstly, the King had to concentrate hard on chocolate cake. It was very difficult for him to remember just what it looked like – the feel and the taste. He had only held a piece of cake in his hand on one occasion: it had been a present from his father on the day he was crowned King. His father had sold of the last of the royal jewels to buy the cake. It had to be specially imported from another Kingdom.

The King thought to himself, "Since the day of my father's coronation, nothing exciting has ever passed our lips in this Kingdom. I am such a failure. If only I could bring the people the dreamy chocolate cake!"

The King put all his energy into dreaming that night. He did not move in his sleep, he simply dreamt. Sure enough, along came the chocolate cake; only this time it was different.

There he was, opening an old chest and inside it was the same chocolate cake. He knelt down and ate from the chest. He ate and ate and ate. The chocolate cake showed no sign of shrinking. How delightful! An everlasting chocolate cake! The King had eaten too much. He was feeling a little sick. He put the lid back on the chest, walked away, came back again and opened the lid. The chocolate cake still sat there, looking just as gooey, just as delicious and... just as whole! He reached out a hand but, before he could take another bite of the cake, he awoke.

Startled, the King recalled the details of the dream. He realised that the old chest was an exact replica of one he had seen before in one of the neglected rooms of his neglected palace. He did not bother dressing but ran straight off to seek out the chest. It was his father's property originally and now that the old King had died it was his son's. However, nothing of any value was ever passed down to the next generation. All the royal family's silver had been sold.

The chest was just where the King had remembered from the dream. It was covered in dust and cobwebs. There was nothing so complicated as a key to open it, the King just jerked the lid open. To his grave disappointment, he did not see a chocolate cake concealed within. Instead, the chest was full of many layers of mouldy and musty cheap cloth.

"What on earth's use are these?" thought the King. "Why did my father hoard so much rubbish?"

The King continued to trawl through the items inside, wheezing and coughing a little with the dust, until he came to the last layer – a thick layer of sacking. In the sacking, he felt something hard. He pulled the sack from the chest, opened the neck of the bag and looked inside. He could not see clearly so, feeling carefully, he brought forth the contents into the light. There might not be a cake but there might be… the ingredients!

He pulled out some cocoa beans, flour, oil and a little sugar. Last of all, he drew out a small, yellowing piece of paper.

Unfolding it, he recognised his father's handwriting, and read...

DEAR SON,

IF EVER YOU FIND THIS LITTLE TREASURE THEN PERHAPS
YOU MAY LIKE TO TRY DOING SOMETHING WITH IT.
I HID IT HERE BECAUSE I COULD NOT BE BOTHERED
TO FIND A COOK!
I WAS GIVEN THE BAG BY A WANDERING ELF. HE SAID
THE FAIRIES HAD GIVEN HIM THE INGREDIENTS. HE
TOLD ME THEY WOULD MAKE MAGIC IN THE RIGHT
HANDS! (YOU KNOW HOW THESE CRAZY ELVES GET IDEAS
INTO THEIR HEADS!)
YOUR LOVING FATHER

The King put the letter into his pocket. How typical of his father, he thought: too lazy! He had never achieved anything, never seemed to want to; too busy sitting and thinking.

Then the King thought again. Why, nothing had changed! What had he himself done for his people? He was the same type as his father. If only he could bring about some small change, some little flutter of excitement to this kingdom.

Well, *he* could at least *try* to make the cake. However, he could not cook; he had never baked in his life. He needed someone who could be trusted to do a good job. He immediately thought of his personal baker, the lady who stamped the crown on the royal loaf. She was said to be a wonderful cook, her bread the best in the Kingdom – fit for the King. He needed to place this important task in the hands of experience.

This lady, Mari, was now an old lady who had baked all her life. There! That was the plan then. He would take the ingredients to Mari and see if she could indeed perform some kind of magic with them.

## II

Mari stood in the kitchen stirring the brown mixture in a large earthenware bowl. She had ground the cocoa beans then delicately folded in the oil and two of the largest eggs that were ever laid by the royal hens. Next came the sugar and the finely sieved flour. The dark brown paste swished about in the bowl. Mari did not dare dip a finger to taste. The King had sworn her to secrecy - this was to be a very special cake.

Mari had never worked with such ingredients before but she knew from her mother's mother what she should do. Her grandmother had once been a famous cake-maker in another Kingdom where everyone ate lots of cake. Fortunately, she had recorded her recipe and method for future generations.

Mari felt so honoured to be given such an important task. She would take her time so as not to make any mistakes. Carefully she poured the mixture into a round shallow tin then she scraped every last drop of the thick, brown liquid in as well. As she was doing so, the King opened the door of the kitchen.

"Excuse me, Mari, but is it ready yet?" The King's face was full of gleeful expectation.

"No, it is not," said Mari, quite curtly. She would not normally address the King thus but this was *her* kitchen and *her* reputation at stake. "It will be half an hour or so."

The King closed the door. He waited, nervously, like a husband waiting for his wife to have her baby. At last, the half hour was up. He asked again.

"Mari, is it ready *now*?"

Mari said nothing but gave the King a look that made him feel like a naughty little boy. She moved slowly to the large oven and opened the door to peek in. The King bent his head, trying to catch a glimpse of the prize.

"Mari, is it good? Has it finished? Is it a fine cake?"

Mari tut-tutted as she pulled the tin from the oven. It contained a perfectly shaped dark brown sponge, risen to twice its previous height.

Mari saw the King looking and, before he could ask another question, she announced, "The cake is cooked to perfection; more than that I cannot say. We will have to wait for it to cool sufficiently before the tasting. I will decorate the cake with the rest of the ground cocoa and sugar - that will make it more appealing. Please leave me to finish my work. Tell me, your Majesty, where will you be waiting and I shall bring the cake up to you. There is no need for you to 'help' any further."

The King waited in one of the palace rooms. It was not what you could call 'palatial' but it was the best he could manage. An old wooden table stood in the middle of the room; eight chairs set around it. Sitting in the chairs were the King, the queen and five of the most trusted servants. All were to keep the story of the cake to themselves.

Mari stepped carefully into the room, carrying the cake before her on the best plate she could find in the kitchen. She placed the cake in the middle of the table and cut seven slices. There were gasps from those seated.

Each took a slice and as soon as each had finished their first mouthful, there was a murmur of unanimous approval. Everyone nodded hard and made up all sorts of words to explain just how delicious the cake really was.

They sat back licking their lips, the cake all gone. All smiled except for the King, who was looking long and hard at the empty plate. This was very odd behaviour but then this kingdom had been ruled by a long line of very odd Kings. No-one spoke. Mari thought she had better say something.

"Well, that's it! I'm glad you all enjoyed the cake."

Mari, the queen and the servants stood up. The queen nodded and the others departed, leaving her alone with her husband.

"What on earth is wrong with you?" she asked. "Mari bakes a wonderful cake, we all eat it and enjoy

it universally. We congratulate her and smile. You do not smile; instead, you have a lost look on your face and stare at the empty plate."

For a moment, the King said nothing. Then, slowly, he recovered his voice.

"The cake – it should have come back again. It should have been an everlasting chocolate cake."

The queen looked at him in complete disbelief.

"Everlasting cake! You are completely crazy – you need a doctor!"

"No," said the King, trying to explain, "I mean in the dream – the cake was everlasting in the dream. Once I had eaten one piece, I could have another and another and the cake was always the same – it was always whole. Only half of the dream is true. Yes, we have found the chocolate cake, or rather the ingredients for the cake, but it is not an everlasting cake!"

Now the queen understood. However, she was not going to be upset by a dream and a chocolate cake that didn't last.

"Ah well," she said, "you know what they say my dear –'you can't have your cake and eat it'."

The King was not amused.

### III

By that afternoon, the King had recovered a little. He was relaxing - playing cards with the queen. Without warning, Mari burst in upon the royal couple.

"Begging your pardons, your Majesties," she said, breathlessly, "but something of strange wonder has happened beneath this very palace roof! Right here in the kitchen – come quickly and see!"

Mari ran off to the kitchen, the King and queen in hot pursuit.

"There!" she said, "Look!"

There on the table lay the sack from the chest.

"The sack is full of ingredients. Yesterday there was not a drop of oil, a cocoa bean or a grain of flour. It's a miracle!"

The King was ecstatic.

"Yes, Mari, it is a miracle... and be prepared for more!"

Then he told Mari all about the dream of the everlasting cake described in his father's note.

"Your hands are magic hands, Mari!" and he laughed out loud.

The King told Mari that they must go into full speed chocolate cake production. It was his dream come true. The people of this small Kingdom could have a taste of riches, each and every one of them. The population of the Kingdom only numbered about one thousand. There would be a lot of baking to do!

Mari told the King that the people would have to be patient; she could not bake the hundred or so cakes needed in one day. She would do her very best, she said.

"However, with more tins, another oven or two

and a few helpers, who knows what I might be able to achieve!"

They worked hard all day. Then Mari made another strange discovery. Only she was able to mix the ingredients to produce the cakes. If a helper attempted to mix then there was no mixture – the ingredients remained separated in the bowl. There was indeed something magical between Mari and the cakes; no-one else possessed that magical touch.

Still, the helpers were useful in turning the mixture out into the tins and levelling them off. They put the tins into the ovens, checked the cooking time and collected the finished product.

By the end for the first week, cake production had reached one hundred and twenty each day. The people were so happy. Never before had they tasted such riches. Now they could taste those riches each and every day!

The King called a special meeting with Mari. He was concerned for her. Would she be able to keep up the cake making? He politely pointed out that she was no longer a youngster. Could she stand the strain?

However, Mari was confident. She told the King that she could manage perfectly well, thank you very much.

Things were fine for a while. The people rejoiced under the King's new slogan 'Let them eat cake!' However, not only did some eat their own share but also began to eat the share of others. There were

reports of cake theft during the day and more often at night. There were rumours that there was extra cake about and people began to ask for double or triple their share. There were fights for cake in the street. There was such greed amongst the people for more and more and still more cake that the kingdom was falling into chaos.

"There is only one answer – we must step up production!" said the King. "I will ask Mari if we can do so."

Mari said that this was not a problem.

More cake was distributed amongst the people and for a time they were content. Then the chaos broke out again. More cake came along. However, each time the people received it, they ended up wanting more. It was bound to end in disaster… and so it did.

So exhausted was Mari from cooking over two hundred chocolate cakes a day that she decided she must go to bed early one night. She never woke up. She died from too much hard work. The doctor said it was the chocolate cake that killed her.

The secret of the cake making, the skill of her magic hands, all had died with her.

The King expected the people to riot. They had no more chocolate cake; no more little riches in life. Instead, the opposite happened. With no more chocolate cake, there was nothing left to fight over. Order was restored. People were nice to each other again. It was as if there had never been any chocolate cake in the first place.

"What more do we really need than our simple bread?" the people said. "We have discovered that we do not need these riches. They do not help us. Instead, they make us fight and we are unhappy. Now we are happy with just our bread."

The King was happy too. Perhaps he had not been such a bad King after all. He too would go back to his bread. He would miss only one thing – the crown stamp upon his morning loaf!